P9-APY-681

A Note to Parents and Caregivers:

Read-it! Readers are for children who are just starting on the amazing road to reading. These beautiful books support both the acquisition of reading skills and the love of books.

 The PURPLE LEVEL presents basic topics and objects using high frequency words and simple language patterns.

 The RED LEVEL presents familiar topics using common words and repeating sentence patterns.

 The BLUE LEVEL presents new ideas using a larger vocabulary and varied sentence structure.

 The YELLOW LEVEL presents more challenging ideas, a broad vocabulary, and wide variety in sentence structure.

 The GREEN LEVEL presents more complex ideas, an extended vocabulary range, and expanded language structures.

 The ORANGE LEVEL presents a wide range of ideas and concepts using challenging vocabulary and complex language structures.

When sharing a book with your child, read in short stretches, pausing often to talk about the pictures. Have your child turn the pages and point to the pictures and familiar words. And be sure to reread favorite stories or parts of stories.

There is no right or wrong way to share books with children. Find time to read with your child, and pass on the legacy of literacy.

Adria F. Klein, Ph.D.
Professor Emeritus
California State University
San Bernardino, California

Editor: Christianne Jones
Page Production: Tracy Davies
Creative Director: Keith Griffin
Editorial Director: Carol Jones
Managing Editor: Catherine Neitge

First American edition published in 2006 by
Picture Window Books
5115 Excelsior Boulevard
Suite 232
Minneapolis, MN 55416
877-845-8392
www.picturewindowbooks.com

Copyright © 2004 by Allegra Publishing Limited
Unit 13/15 Quayside Lodge
William Morris Way
Townmead Road
London SW6 2UZ
UK

All rights reserved. No part of this book may be reproduced without written
permission from the publisher. The publisher takes no responsibility for the use of
any of the materials or methods described in this book, nor for the products thereof.

The art in this book was colored by Datagraph System.

Printed in the United States of America.

Library of Congress Cataloging-in-Publication Data
Law, Felicia.
Rumble meets Wally Warthog / by Felicia Law ; illustrated by Yoon-Mi Pak.— 1st
American ed.
p. cm. — (Read-it! readers)
Summary: When a guest staying at Rumble's Cave Hotel asks the chef, Chester,
many questions about the food and how it is prepared, Shelby sets out to learn
whether the guest is a spy.
ISBN 1-4048-1289-X (hard cover)
[1. Cookery—Fiction. 2. Hotels, motels, etc.—Fiction. 3. Warthog—Fiction.
4. Dragons—Fiction. 5. Spiders—Fiction.] I. Pak, Yoon-Mi, ill. II. Title. III. Series.

PZ7.L41835Rumw 2005
[E]—dc22   2005007364

Rumble Meets
Wally Warthog

by Felicia Law
illustrated by Yoon-Mi Pak

Special thanks to our advisers for their expertise:

Adria F. Klein, Ph.D.
Professor Emeritus, California State University
San Bernardino, California

Susan Kesselring, M.A.
Literacy Educator
Rosemount–Apple Valley–Eagan (Minnesota) School District

PiCTURE WiNDOW BOOKS
Minneapolis, Minnesota

This is a story of a cool, young dragon named Rumble. When his grandma leaves her run-down cave to him, Rumble sets about making it into a four-star hotel. He doesn't do it all alone. He has help from a picky hotel inspector and an annoying spider named Shelby.

Rumble has hired a chef named
Chester and opened a restaurant
in Rumble's Cave Hotel.
Nobody knows if the chef is
any good, but when a strange
guest comes to breakfast, lunch,
AND dinner, it looks as if he
will be put to the test.

"Good morning, sir," said Rumble. "Welcome to Rumble's Cave Hotel."

"Good morning," said Wally Warthog. "I need a room for two nights."

"You've come to the right place," said Rumble. "We have a room for two nights."

"That will be four pennies," said Shelby Spider. "Please pay here."

7

"I'm here to eat in your restaurant. I need the best table, the best waiter, and the best food," said Wally. "I'll need breakfast and lunch. Yes, I'll need a healthy lunch."

"And supper?" asked Rumble.

"Of course," said Wally. "I'll need a delicious supper, too. In fact, I shall need to eat a lot."

"A lot?" repeated Shelby. "But you're too fat already!"

"What did the spider say?" asked Wally.

"She said she has a new cat called Freddy," Rumble said.

"Shhh!" Rumble said to Shelby. "Don't be rude to the guests. Go count your pennies!"

Wally sat down for breakfast. He read the breakfast menu.

Porridge with milk and sugar
Milk with sugar and porridge
Sugar with porridge and milk

"Hmmm!" he snuffled. "A difficult choice! Is the porridge thick or runny?" he asked Chester the chef. "Is it smooth or lumpy?"

"The porridge is cooked just right," said Chester. "One lump or two?"

13

At noon, Wally sat down for lunch. He read the lunch menu.

First course

Porridge left over from breakfast

Second course

Meat
and
Vegetables

Third course

Porridge left over from breakfast
with jam

"Hmmm!" he snorted. "Give me the meat. I'll pass on the porridge."

"Is the meat fried?" asked Wally. "Is it roasted? Is it boiled? Is it grilled?"

"All four," said Chester. "I cook it over and over again until someone eats it."

"Excellent!" said Wally. "I like my meat well done."

"Are the vegetables raw or cooked?" asked Wally. "Are they fresh? Are they washed?"

"The vegetables are fine," said Chester. "The snails seem to like them."

Chester looked at Wally carefully. He sure asks a lot of questions, Chester thought.

"The warthog is asking a lot of questions," Chester told Rumble. "I think he's a spy."

"He's our guest," said Rumble. "He can ask what he likes."

"As long as he pays," said Shelby.

"He has a pencil," said Chester. "He's writing on the menu."

"He's our guest," said Rumble. "He can write what he likes."

"As long as he pays," repeated Shelby.

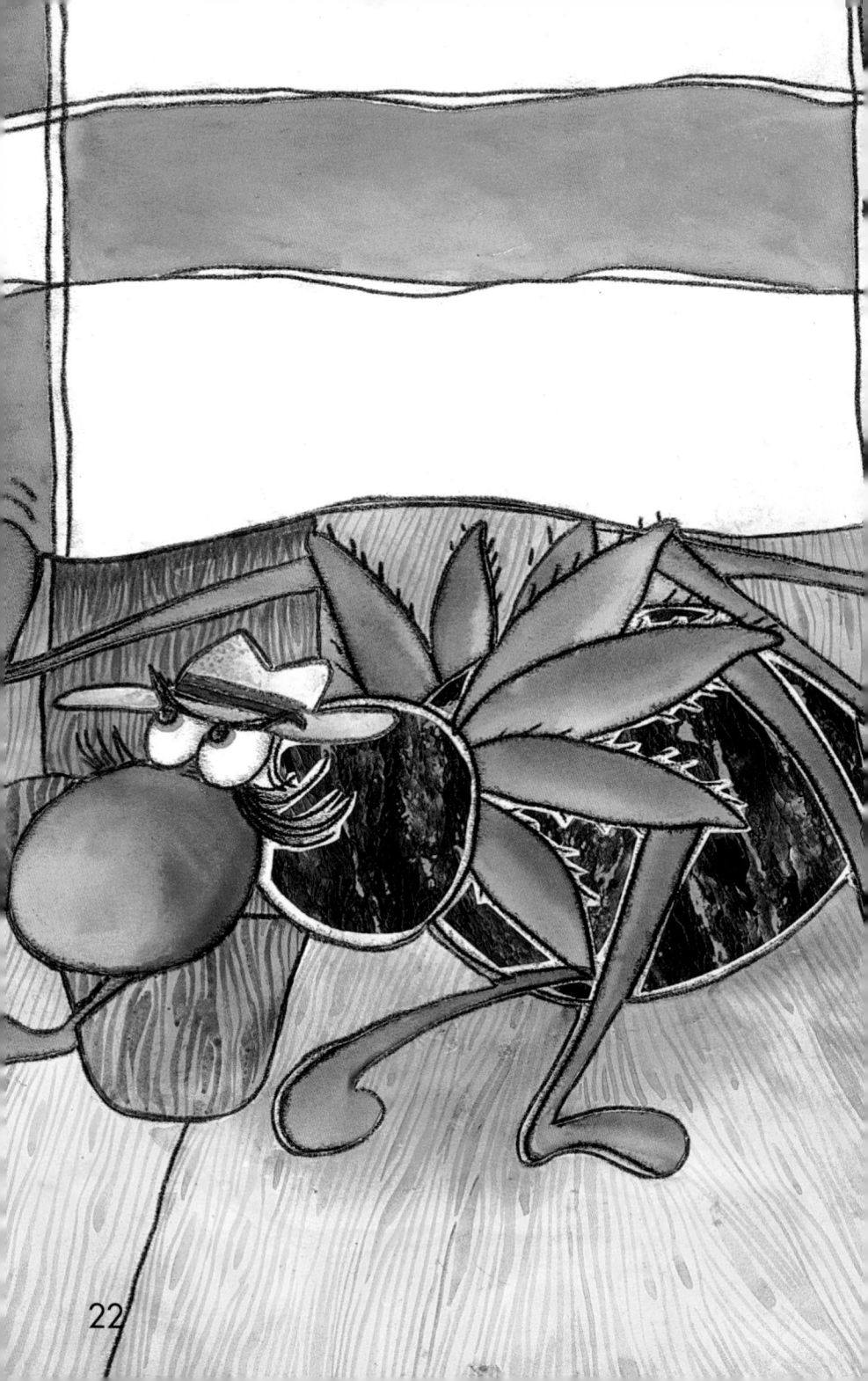

"That warthog is a spy," repeated Chester. "He's asking a lot of questions, he's writing on the menu, and he's stealing my recipes."

"Fine," said Shelby. "I'll creep under the table and find out what he's doing."

"Remember—he's a guest," hissed Rumble.

"Remember—he's a spy," hissed Chester.

Shelby crept under the table. She crept over Wally's foot, up his leg, across his knee, around the edge of the tablecloth, and hid in his napkin.

She was good at creeping, and she was a good spy. Soon, Shelby had her answer.

"He's writing about your food," Shelby reported to Chester. "He's writing in a secret notebook, and he's saying some very rude things. He says your porridge is too lumpy. He says your gravy is too runny."

"He's a food critic," said Chester. "I hate food critics!"

ridge   too thick, too salty,
      too cold

milk   too sour, too wet

sugar   too sweet, too crunchy

vegetable   too mushy, too smooth

meat   too peppery, too dry

jam   too lumpy, too bitter

gravy   too hot, too greasy, too ru

...

chef : needs more practic

manager: tries too hard

price   too many pe

"He says you need practice," said Shelby. "He'll give the restaurant a silver knife and fork award instead of a gold one."

"A silver knife and fork award!" cried Rumble. "A silver knife and fork award for the restaurant is just fine."

TONIGHT
– Specialty of the Chef –
Porridge

"A silver knife and fork award is not fine! I should get the GOLD knife and fork award. I practice my porridge every day!" Chester yelled.

Rumble and Shelby could only smile. They did eat a lot of porridge.

More *Read-it!* Readers

Bright pictures and fun stories help you practice your reading skills. Look for more books at your level.

Happy Birthday, Gus! by Jacklyn Williams
Happy Easter, Gus! by Jacklyn Williams
Happy Halloween, Gus! by Jacklyn Williams
Happy Thanksgiving, Gus! by Jacklyn Williams
Happy Valentine's Day, Gus! by Jacklyn Williams
Matt Goes to Mars by Carole Tremblay
Merry Christmas, Gus! by Jacklyn Williams
Rumble Meets Buddy Beaver by Felicia Law
Rumble Meets Eli Elephant by Felicia Law
Rumble Meets Keesha Kangaroo by Felicia Law
Rumble Meets Penny Panther by Felicia Law
Rumble Meets Wally Warthog by Felicia Law

Looking for a specific title or level? A complete list of *Read-it!* Readers is available on our Web site:
www.picturewindowbooks.com